A Place
for Joey

A Place for Joey

Carol Flynn Harris

Boyds Mills Press

Text copyright © 2001 by Carol Flynn Harris

Boyds Mills Press, Inc.
A Highlights Company
815 Church Street
Honesdale, Pennsylvania 18431
Printed in the United States of America

U.S. Cataloging-in-Publication Data
   (Library of Congress Standards)

Harris, Carol Flynn.
   A Place for Joey / by Carol Flynn Harris. — 1st ed.
   [160] p. ; cm.
Summary: In this novel set in early 20th-century Boston, a family of Italian
immigrants work hard to attain their dream—a farm in the country—but their
son Joey can't bear to leave the city.
   ISBN 1-56397-108-9 hc • 1-59078-284-4 pb
   1. Boston — History — 20th century — Fiction. 2. Boston — Emigration
and immigration — Fiction. I. Title.
   813.54 [F] 21 2001 CIP AC
   00-107759

First edition, 2001
First Boyds Mills Press paperback edition, 2004
The text of this book is set in 13-point Sabon.

10 9 8 7 6 5 4 3 2   hc
10 9 8 7 6 5 4 3 2 1 pb

*To George
for his love, patience, and support and to
everyone in the Newton Monday Night
Writers' Group for their encouragement,
enthusiasm, and expertise.*

Thanks to

The North End elders, whose recollections in Anthony
Riccio's *Portraits of an Italian-American
Neighborhood* enlightened and inspired.

And to Donna Wells of the Boston Police Department
and Jack Zollo of the Watertown Historical Society
for research assistance.

Chapter One

JOEY CALABRO LAY IN HIS COT beside the window in the kitchen. He listened to Mama talking to his big brother Luigi and Papa in Italian.

"Another day with no snow, thank God! Every day you can work outside, our money grows faster. Soon we'll be able to buy our own land!"

Land! *La terra!* Joey hated the sound of that word whether it was spoken in Italian or English.

Every morning he woke up smelling the aroma of strong coffee and the salami sandwiches Mama made for the lunch pails. Every morning he heard Mama's voice and the voices of Papa and Luigi. Every morning the talk was the same. *La terra!*

Buying land meant moving. Why am I the only one in my family who wants to stay in the North End? Joey wondered for the hundredth time. Why doesn't anybody care what I want? And why do they always have to speak in Italian? Mama, Papa, and Luigi didn't even try using English anymore.

"We'll have chickens," Luigi's soft voice murmured. "Someday we'll have a pig."

"I'll grow broccoli and Swiss chard." Joey heard Papa's words and could almost see his smile. "We'll have grapevines beside the house."

"Just like in Italy," Mama said.

But we don't live in Italy anymore, Joey said to himself. We live in America. He pulled the blanket over his head. He heard the *clomp, clomp* of two pairs of boots echoing down the wooden stairway.

Joey turned over in his narrow cot and prayed to St. Francis of Assisi. I don't care how cold you make it, he begged. I won't complain. Just make it snow. Then there'll be no more construction work for Papa and Luigi. Maybe the snow will be so deep that Mama won't be able to go to work at the candy factory. The money in the Postal Savings book won't grow. And we won't ever move away.

Joey scraped his fingernail on the frosty window and peered out. No snow. St. Francis must be on Mama's side. She had grown up in Assisi, after all.

Mama spoke to Joey in Italian all the time he was eating his bread. "Giuseppe, I had to mend your trousers again last night. I want you to be careful what you put in your pockets. Every time I look there's another hole. I'm going to give you a dollar eighty-five cents today. On your way home from school, you stop by Mr. Venezia's and get olive oil." She shook her finger. "Don't go to Mr. Parrello for the oil. He charges a nickel more a gallon. Get tomatoes from Mr. Carlo. Tell him I don't want mushy ones." His mother poked him with a wooden spoon. "Giuseppe, are you listening to me?"

"I'm listening." Joey pocketed the handful of change Mama had carefully counted out from the jar on the shelf over the stove. "Don't call me Giuseppe, Mama. Call me Joey. That's my American name." He chewed his finger and leaned across the table. "Mama, I don't wanna move to a farm in Watertown."

Mama picked up Rosa. She brushed the two-year-old's straight brown hair and continued talking to Joey. "Come right home after you do the errands. I need you to scrub the stairs and watch the baby while I make gravy. No playing ball in the streets or hanging around the waterfront like a hoodlum. Do you hear me, Giuseppe?"

"Ma, you didn't listen to me!"

"Don't call me Ma. Show some respect." Mama swatted Joey with the dishtowel, brushed his hair back from his forehead, and planted a kiss on his cheek. "Pay attention in school. Learn from the teacher. Be a good boy."

Joey tromped down the two flights of stairs muttering, "Yeah, yeah, yeah." Mama sure talked a lot, Joey thought. Mostly about things like his being a good boy, respect, and buying land to grow tomatoes. But she never listened. She never heard what he wanted.

He leaned against the side of the tenement next door where his best friend, Domenic Bonano, lived. He took a deep breath. The yeasty aroma of bread from the bakery on the first floor blended with the salty breeze from the waterfront. Joey could even hear the magical, metallic squeal of the elevated train down on Commercial Street beside the harbor. He closed his eyes and listened to Mr. Venezia, the grocer, calling out to Mr. Russo in the meat market next door. "How much a pound for your beef today, Pasquale?"

He heard the clip-clop of horse's hooves and the rumble of wooden wagon wheels on the cobbled street. He inhaled the flavor of gravy coming from an open window over the grocery store. Whenever

Uncle Vincenzo took them out to the country to see the land, all Joey could hear was chickens cackling. All he could smell was pigs.

"Hey, Joey!"

Joey jumped, opened his eyes, and saw Domenic grinning at him.

"Wake up, what are you sleeping for in the day?" Domenic chewed on a piece of bread as he talked. "Wanna go down to the waterfront after school? See if there's any tankers there?" His smile got wider. "Listen to the sailors swear?"

Joey smiled back. "Yeah! And we could play baseball in the freight yard." Then he felt the coins jingle in his pocket. He slowly shook his head. "But I can't. My mother wants me to—" Joey stopped. All of a sudden he pictured the farmland in Watertown where he'd be moving pretty soon. What would he do for fun there? he wondered glumly. Watch the tomatoes grow?

"Domenic, I justa got an idea," Joey said, stumbling over his English as he did when he got nervous. "I'm no gonna go to school today."

His friend stared. "You mean you're gonna hook school?"

Joey nodded. "I'm gonna hook."

"Hey! I'll hook too!" Domenic grinned. "If my mother finds out I didn't go to school, she's gonna kill me." Domenic looked around nervously. "We better get outta here before she sees me. C'mon." Joey raced to keep up as his friend ran up the street toward North Square. Domenic finally sat down on the curb, juggling apples he had swiped from under a pushcart. "Then if she tells my father when he gets home, he's gonna kill me too," he said.

"How can he kill you if you're already dead, *stupidi?*" Joey grabbed an apple. What would happen to him if Mama found out? He didn't want to think about it. He took a bite of the apple and spit it out the way he'd seen Uncle Vincenzo do when he chewed a cigar. "I don't care if my mother kills me," he said, tossing the rotten apple away. "I'd rather be dead than live in Watertown."

"Watertown's not so bad," Domenic said. "My uncle Nick works at this big factory there—the same one your uncle Vincenzo works at. Uncle Nick came here at Christmas. He brought candy bars for all us kids, a scarf for my mother, and a new pipe for my father. I bet your uncle makes even more money than my uncle does. Your uncle owns a car!"

"My father and Luigi aren't gonna be working in the factory when we move," Joey said. "Where we're gonna be you can't even see the factory. There's no sidewalks, no people, no nothing." He sighed. "It's justa like where my mother came from in Italy."

Domenic laughed. "You sound like my father sometimes the way you talk."

"*Just* like," Joey corrected himself. "What are you laughing for anyway? Your father speaks good English like me."

Joey was proud that he sounded like Domenic's father. Mr. Bonano had come over a long time ago. Domenic and his brothers and sisters were born right here in the North End. Nobody in his family talked about moving away, Joey thought. Nobody in the North End wants to move away except Mama, Papa, and Luigi.

Domenic poked Joey's arm. "We gotta get outta here. If somebody who knows my mother sees me, I'm gonna be killed."

"You're dead for sure, then! Everyone in the North End knows your mother." Joey raced down North Street to catch up with his friend. For once he was glad that his mother wasn't like Mrs. Bonano. Mama didn't visit or chat on the sidewalk like everyone else in the neighborhood.

He followed Domenic as he zigzagged through the narrow streets. They headed down the hill to the waterfront and finally stopped at the lamppost on Commercial Street.

"Beat you!" Domenic yelled.

"So? I'll beat you to the molasses tank!" Joey

dashed across the wide street, dodging horse-drawn wagons. Breathing hard, he leaned against the wire fence surrounding the huge steel tank that dominated the waterfront.

"What took you so long?" he asked Domenic, who reached the tank seconds after he did.

"No fair. I slipped on a pile of horse manure. Phew! It stinks!" Domenic wiped his hands on his pants.

"*Stupidi!*" Joey said, and laughed.

So did a guy in overalls standing inside the fence smoking a cigarette.

Joey glanced at him. He had an idea. He chewed his finger and blurted out, "Hey mister, could I get a job here at the molasses tank?"

The man in the overalls laughed louder than before. "I wouldn't hire Eye-talians for all the rum that's made from this molasses."

"Get a job?" Domenic squinted at Joey. "Who wants a job?"

Joey gave Domenic a kick in the ankle and moved closer to the fence. "It's justa me," he stammered, pointing to himself. "Not him. Justa me."

The man looked at Domenic. "Your pal don't understand English, does he? Tell him what I said. Tell him I said he's full of that horse manure you fell in. See if he understands that."

"Hey!" Domenic said. "Who do you think you are, you—"

Joey pulled on Domenic's arm. "Come on, let's go. Whatta we care what he says? He's not the boss."

The workman smirked. He sat down and leaned against the tank. "Oh, yeah?"

Domenic gripped the wire fence. "If you're the boss, mister, I'm the mayor of Boston. I'm gonna—" A big, burly man with a clipboard walked from around the side of the tank and scowled at the workman. "Get off your butt, you lazy mick," the big man grunted. "You're paid to do a job."

The workman stood up and ground out his cigarette with his boot. "I ain't one of them no-good Irish," he muttered.

"I'm gonna call old Mayor Fitzgerald and tell him you said Irish are no good!" Domenic yelled.

He and Joey ran down the street, laughing at the workman's curses. "How come you asked him about a job?" Domenic asked when they stopped to catch their breath in front of an abandoned warehouse. "You gotta be fourteen to quit school."

Joey tapped his head. "Stupid. I shouldda known he wasn't the boss." Domenic was his best friend, but he didn't feel like talking about his idea right now.

"*Stupidi*," Domenic agreed. "That guy was a

dope. Besides, our mothers wouldn't let us quit anyway. Let's get outta here, go back to North Street, and . . . " He stopped and poked Joey. Two kids with turned-up coat collars were walking quickly toward them. "Whadda they want?" he whispered.

The larger of the two boys advanced on Domenic, not stopping until Domenic had his back pressed against the wall of the building.

"I heard what you said back there," the kid said, gesturing toward the molasses tank. "So you think Irish are no good, huh?"

Domenic shook his head. He tried to move. The kid clapped a big fist on his shoulder.

Joey stepped forward. He tried to keep his voice from shaking. "He no say that."

"Nobody's talking to you!" The other kid, a redhead, put out his hand and pushed Joey against the wall. "You just shut up and listen to what's gonna happen to your bigmouthed pal here." He turned to his sidekick. "Tell him, Sully."

Sully grabbed Domenic's jacket. "Here's what we do to wops who hang out on our turf and bad-mouth the Irish."

"Hey, you ripped my jacket!" Domenic yelled.

"You'll get more than your jacket ripped if you don't shut your—"

"What's going on over here?"

Four heads turned to see a tall, blue-coated policeman bearing down on them.

Sully let go of Domenic and grinned a toothy smile at the policeman. "Nothing, Officer Maloney," he said.

"That's all it better be, Sullivan. And you too, buddy boy," the policeman said, looking at the red-head. He pointed a large finger at Domenic. "What do you have to say about this?" he asked.

Joey grabbed Domenic's arm. "*Dai, scorri!*" he shouted.

Joey and Domenic heard the policeman yelling as they raced away. "Hey, you two, come back here!"

Chapter Two

"GEEZ, JOEY," DOMENIC SAID, panting. He sank down on the bags of potatoes outside Carlo's grocery store. "I thought I was a goner! Look! That no-good Irish bully ripped my jacket. My mother's gonna kill me."

Joey stretched out on the sidewalk and leaned his head against the lumpy sacks. He blew in and out, trying to catch his breath. "We no do anything to them!"

"Why'd you yell 'run' in Italian?" Domenic asked.

"'Cause they were Irish, *stupidi*," Joey said. "They don't understand Italian."

"But I was just gonna tell the cop what they did."

Joey rolled his eyes. "*Stupidi!*" he said again. "Didn't you hear him call the red-headed kid Buddy? Those Irish, they all stick together. That cop was going to make you look like the bad guy."

Domenic scratched his head. "Yeah," he said, slowly. "You're right, Joey. He did know those guys, didn't he?"

"He knew them all right," Joey said. "You heard what those Irish called us, didn't you?"

"Yeah, bad names. For no reason. Well, how's this?" Domenic said. "I know some bad names for them." He stood up and hollered as loud as he could. "Thick mick! Harp!"

Joey laughed, but then his smile faded. "Ooh, Domenic, you better watch your mouth. Those Irish are after you."

Domenic put out his hand. "Hey, together we can take them. Right, Joey?"

"Right," Joey answered. But he wasn't really sure they could. And what would Domenic do if he was alone when he ran into those Irish again? Sometimes his friend *did* have a big mouth.

Unless he could get a job and stay here, big trouble could come to Domenic. Another reason for not going to Watertown, he told himself. Domenic needs me.

The next day, Joey tried to forget his worries. It was Saturday, and Saturdays were for playing kick-the-can in the street. Saturdays were for not thinking about anything except having a good time.

But Sunday came after Saturday. Sunday meant getting dressed up in his scratchy, starched shirt, serge pants, and stiff shoes and going to Mass with Mama and Rosa. Having to sit as still as the statue of the Sacred Heart unless he wanted a poke in the ribs. But on this Sunday, Mama didn't even glare at him when he sat back in the pew instead of kneeling up straight. Today Mama was thinking of only one thing.

"Giuseppe, be a good boy and help me," she told him when they got home from Mass. "Your uncle Vincenzo will be here soon. He doesn't like to wait. Pack the bread that Cousin Felix likes."

Joey wrapped the warm, crusty loaves in brown paper, but even the sweet aroma of Mama's home-made bread couldn't make this Sunday go away.

"Who cares what Cousin Felix likes?" Joey mumbled under his breath. "If Cousin Felix didn't have land to sell we could stay right here."

When Mama left the room, Joey snitched an olive from the basket she had packed and looked at himself in the smoky mirror over the trunk. He narrowed his dark eyes and scowled. I could pass for fourteen, he thought. "I bet I could get a job right now," he muttered. "I could work at the molasses tank or anywhere I want, no matter what that stupid guy said. Nobody would be treating me bad if I had money in my pocket. I could go down to the social club at night. I'd buy the newspaper and read it out loud to the men who can't read English. I'd get respect." Joey pushed his hair over his eyes and practiced a sneer like the boss at the molasses tank.

"Why are you looking like that? Are you sick?"

Joey jumped. Mama stood in the doorway staring at him. She came over and brushed the hair back from his face and felt his forehead with the back of her hand.

For a second Joey thought about saying he didn't feel good, but Mama would make him take awful-tasting medicine and hang a bag of garlic around his neck to keep sickness away. Since Rosa almost died from the influenza last year, she worried all the time. He sighed. "I'm okay. Where are Papa and Luigi?"

"They went to get a cigar for Uncle Vincenzo." Mama looked out the window. "Here's your uncle now. Look! Everyone's coming over to see his car." She patted Joey's hair again. "Take the basket. I'll get Rosa and the blankets. We're on our way to

Watertown." His mother kissed the cross she wore on a gold chain around her neck. "And pretty soon we'll be staying there. For good!"

Joey lifted the basket from the kitchen table and hoisted it onto his shoulder. "Not me," he muttered. He looked around the kitchen, from the saints' pictures on the walls to the oilcloth-covered table, from the shiny black stove to his cot with the gray blanket. He scuffed his shoe on the worn wooden floor. He'd scrubbed that floor for his mother since he was big enough to help. He looked through the doorway to where Mama, Papa, and Rosa slept. Through the other narrow doorway, Joey could see the room where Luigi and their boarder, Antonio Rizzo, slept. In December Antonio had gone back to Italy to work for the winter. Joey could sleep in that room now if he wanted to, but he liked his cot in the kitchen better.

Joey remembered how welcome this kitchen seemed to him after the long voyage on the crowded ship. He remembered smiling faces bringing food when he and his family had arrived at this good place. Neighbors had put fruit, bread, and wine on the table. "*Benvenuto!*" they'd all said. One little boy his own age had smiled at him and said an English word that sounded strange but nice. It wasn't long before Joey learned more English from the other kids and the teachers at school. He found out that the little boy was named Domenic and the word he had said was "Welcome!" It was one of the first English words he learned.

Mama thought he should remember Italy, but he didn't. All he remembered was the darkness of a swaying, pitching boat, grown-ups moaning, food that was rotten, and the smell of vomit.

If he thought any more about leaving this safe place, he might cry like he did all the way from Italy. He hadn't cried once since his family got to America seven years ago. He hadn't had anything to cry about.

"What's the matter with you?" Mama came out of the bedroom with Rosa on her hip. "What are you standing there for? Uncle Vincenzo is waiting."

Joey shifted the basket to his other shoulder. He stomped down the two flights behind Mama.

Joey tried to smile back at Rosa, who was laughing and jabbering in her baby talk. "Say like me," he prompted his sister. "My name is Rosy. I'm a big girl." The baby chattered, but what she said didn't sound like either English or Italian.

He blew on his hands. St. Francis of Assisi had answered one prayer, anyway. It was freezing cold. Still, half the neighborhood was gathered around the black Model T Ford. Uncle Vincenzo blew the horn, and everyone laughed.

"You must make lotsa money!" Mr. Bonano said, rubbing his sleeve over the shiny hood. "What's a car like this cost, anyway?"

"Four hundred and forty dollars brand-new," Uncle Vincenzo said proudly. "It's only four years old now."

"You do good," Mr. Bonano said. "If I no have all these kids, if I was single like you and my brother-in-law, I'd work in the factory and make big money, too. But I'd buy me a coupe." He grinned at Luigi, who was already in the front seat of the Model T. "You're next, right?" In Italian he asked, "Ready to make money in the factory like your uncle?"

"I'm not going to work in a factory," said Luigi.

Joey almost dropped the basket on the sidewalk when he heard his normally quiet big brother speak in a loud voice that sounded like Mama's. "Papa and me, we're going to work the land."

Mr. Leone from upstairs threw up his hands. "I wouldn't go back to a farm if you gave me a hundred dollars right here in my hand. I almost starved to death on a farm in Abruzzi." He looked around at the neighbors. "That's why we came over here to America, right? Anyway, even over here the farm boss doesn't pay you as much as the factory or the construction boss does."

Luigi stepped out of the car. He pointed to Papa and then to himself. "We're going to be the bosses on our farm. You only get respect when you're the boss."

Mr. Leone tapped the side of his head. "Luigi work too hard," he said in English. "A young man like him needs a girlfriend. He's too serious alla time."

"Luigi no the crazy guy. You are!" Mama jabbed her finger at Mr. Leone as she climbed into the backseat. Joey would have laughed if he hadn't been so unhappy. Mama can speak English okay when she wants too, he thought.

Mr. Bonano lifted one eyebrow. "America's a good country, but Italians still no the bosses here." He clapped Luigi on the back and smiled at Mama and Papa. In Italian he said, "Have a nice day in the country anyway. Enjoy."

Joey watched Mama, Papa, and Luigi smile at each other. He put the basket in the backseat and waggled his fingers at Domenic.

Uncle Vincenzo got behind the wheel. "Hey, you kids, get your hands offa the car! Get offa the running board!"

Mama added her admonitions in Italian. "If you don't get out of the way, this car will run over you like a train! Boom!"

Amid all the chatter Joey heard Domenic's voice. "Pa, they *are* going to buy a farm. Joey told me."

He heard Mr. Bonano reply. "Crazy talk!" He shook his head. "It takes lotsa bucks to buy a farm. Who's got money to do that? Only rich people own a farm. Joey's mama thinks 'cause she come from northern Italy it make her family special. Huh, they gotta work for a boss like everybody here." Then he smiled at Domenic. "So what, though, what you gonna do? Good luck to them."

Uncle Vincenzo pressed the horn again. Joey tried to enjoy the envy on the faces of Domenic and his friends as the touring car pulled slowly away from the curb into the narrow street. It was hard to smile. He scrunched down in the backseat and ignored Rosa, who wanted to play patty-cake. He groaned to himself. Mama was telling Uncle Vincenzo they almost had the money to pay for the land.

Mama patted Luigi's shoulder. "My Luigi works so hard since we came over. He never got to play like this one does." She smiled at Joey and spread a second blanket over his legs.

"I didn't want to play," Luigi said from the front seat. "I was grown up when we left Italy. I was thirteen. I was older than Giuseppe is now."

Joey slid further down. Was it his fault he was only five when they came to America?

"Vincenzo, your sister knows one thousand ways to feed a family and still save money. Even though hers is the best, I never want to taste macaroni and beans again!" Papa laughed a loud happy laugh. So did Mama, Luigi, and Uncle Vincenzo. So did Rosa.

Joey looked out the window. He saw churches that didn't have crosses on the top. They were stern looking, and they weren't tall like the church on Salem Street.

He listened to the grown-ups chatter about buying seeds and fixing up the old house that was on the land Cousin Felix was selling to them. He heard Mama and Uncle Vincenzo talking about the farm where they grew up in the old country and how beautiful it was.

"The soil in Watertown—it's even better. Cousin Felix says everything grows like God plants the seeds Himself." Papa said.

You'd think it was Papa's family that had owned a farm once to hear him talk, Joey thought. Mama's dream of a farm had them all crazy. He tuned out the Italian, and the questions in his head came through in English. Was he brave enough to tell Mama he was going to leave school, get a job, and stay in the North End? Or was he just going to be a baby like Rosa and go wherever the family went?

He stared glumly through the dusty window at Watertown Square and the cold-looking gray river he could see from the bridge. There were lots of trucks on the street, and the people on the sidewalks all looked like they had someplace to go. Nobody was just standing around talking. There were brick buildings, factories, stores, and houses just like in the North End. But it didn't look the same. The streets were wide and the buildings weren't all close together. It didn't look like a neighborhood. Joey saw only a few kids. One of them had red hair and freckles like the kid named Buddy down on the waterfront. The other one looked like the punk named Sullivan.

Soon the houses got farther and farther apart. Joey didn't see any people at all now. The Model T creaked slowly up a hill. Joey saw fields and rocks covered with a dusting of snow.

Mama pressed her face against the window. "There's the farmhouse we're going to live in!"

Joey saw a shabby, brown house surrounded by bare trees in a frozen field. "Ugly," he muttered under his breath.

"Oh, it'll be so pretty when it's painted yellow," Mama said. "You're going to make some shutters, right, Sal?"

Papa nodded. He pointed out the window. "My

grapevines will be right on the side."

"See those trees?" Luigi peered out. "In the spring they have white blossoms, then apples better than they sell from the pushcarts in Boston."

"The beets, beans, and broccoli will be over there." Mama waved her hands.

Papa raised his finger. "Don't forget the swiss chard!"

Joey stared at the frozen dirt.

"The sign outside will say CALABRO FARM—FRESH, HOME-GROWN PRODUCE." Mama said.

Luigi and Papa nodded and smiled.

Joey looked out the window again. He couldn't see what Mama, Papa, and Luigi saw. He closed his eyes. In his mind he practiced saying, "Have you got any jobs here, mister? I'm fourteen and I can work hard."

"Giuseppe, are you asleep? Get out of the car. What are you dreaming about?"

"Nothing, Mama," Joey lied.

Chapter Three

"I'M GONNA HOOK SCHOOL AGAIN TODAY," Joey told Domenic the next morning. "Wanna come?"

"You're not gonna go down to the waterfront, are you?" Domenic grabbed Joey's arm. "Those Irish kids will be looking for us."

Joey crossed his fingers. "Nah, I won't go there."

"Good." Domenic said. "'Cause I don't dare hook today—not 'cause I don't wanna. I'm not scared of those Irish, Joey, honest! But there's a novena starts tonight at Saint Leonard's. Somebody like Angleo's mother might say, 'Hey, Mrs. Bonano,

Angelo said Domenic wasn't in school today.' Then I'll get—"

"Killed," Joey finished.

Domenic nodded. "You're lucky you go to Sacred Heart. Almost everybody else in our class goes to Saint Leonard's."

"I'd still skip even if we went to Saint Leonard's," Joey said with a swagger. "Even if my mother was going to a novena tonight."

Domenic shook his head. "You're getting tough, Joey." He grinned. "So, what was it like riding in your uncle's car? If he comes again will you ask him to take me for a ride? I've only been in a car once, when—"

"My uncle only gets that car once in a while," Joey interrupted again. "Seven other guys own that car with him. Mama was so mad at Uncle Vincenzo for spending the money it's a wonder you didn't hear her yelling. He's supposed to be saving for the farm like she is. But he's taken us to Watertown twice, so now she's not mad at him anymore." As soon as he said the words he wanted to take them back. Mama said never to tell family business outside the house. But Domenic wasn't listening anyway. He just kept talking about cars.

"My father said this rich guy in Boston comes into the restaurant sometimes. The headwaiter told my father this guy owns a car that has a toilet inside."

Joey laughed. "You tell some big lies, Domenic. No automobile has a toilet in it."

"I'm not lying. This rich guy ordered it special so when he needs to pee he just goes in the backseat. That's where the toilet is."

Joey threw up his hands. "You're crazy, Domenic Bonano! Your father has a good job, but even in your building you have to go out in the hallway and wait in line to pee, just like everybody does."

"This guy's a millionaire, I'm telling you. Ask my father. He'll tell you I'm not lying. Hey, did I tell you that my brother Frankie might give me his harmonica?"

Joey laughed again. Domenic told the best stories of anybody he knew.

"I gotta go," Domenic said when they got to Charter Street. "You won't go down the waterfront, will you, Joey?" he said with a worried look.

Joey shook his head. "No," he said.

Domenic waved as he ran toward the Eliot School.

Joey waited till Domenic was out of sight. Then he walked down Copp's Hill toward the harbor. He hated having to lie to his friend, but the waterfront was where the jobs were. He looked around carefully for Sully and Buddy or any other Irish kids who might be hooking school. No matter how tough Domenic thought he was getting, Joey didn't want to run into any of them when he was alone. He wished his friend were with him. He wished Domenic were going to quit school and get a job, too. He turned his head to make sure there was nobody on the street. The only people he saw were some women and little babies.

"Hey, watch where yer goin'!"

Joey bumped into a tall policeman coming around the corner of Commercial Street.

"*Mi scusi, Signore,*" Joey said, lapsing into Italian in his fright. Geez! It was the same cop they'd run from the other day. "*Aiutami, San Francesco, ti prego!*" he breathed.

The policeman squinted at him. "You don't speak English?"

"Yeah, yeah, I do, Mr. Policeman. Excuse me, please, for bumping you. It was an accident," Joey said carefully.

"It better be," the policeman said. "Shouldn't you be in school?"

He doesn't remember me, Joey thought. Thank you, St. Francis, he said to himself this time. "No, no, uh, I no go to school. I work," he said.

The policeman twirled his stick. "Yer pretty small for fourteen. Where do you work?"

Joey hesitated a minute, pretending he couldn't hear over the sound of the overhead trains. He tried to think what story Domenic would make up. He pointed across the street where the molasses tank gleamed in the sunlight. "I work there, Mr. Policeman, uh, Officer. At the tank." Joey was glad the lie came out in perfect English.

"Yeah, sure you do," the policeman said. "You look pretty shifty to me. What mischief are you up to, anyway?"

Joey tried not to shake. "Nothing, Mr. Policeman, I mean, Officer," he said slowly.

"I bet. Well, you better be sure I don't see you hanging around here again." He started walking away. Joey heard him mutter, "Foreigners! The mother probably got twelve bambinos younger than him. Probably sends them all out to fetch coal instead of going to school."

Joey raced across Commercial Street toward the huge, shiny tank. "Talk English, you stupid," he muttered to himself. He looked back. The policeman was chatting with a couple of sailors and wasn't looking at him.

Joey kept going down to the freight yard. Three cars were being unloaded.

He chewed his finger, then approached the burly men hauling barrels and crates. They tossed them as if they were light as the puffs of smoke coming out of the fireboat anchored in the harbor. "I want a job," he said. "You need some help?"

One of the men stopped, looked at Joey, and said, "Sure. I could use some help. Get on the other end of this crate and help me pick it up."

Joey ran over, bent down, and put his hands under the bottom of the crate. "Like this?" he asked.

"Yeah. When I say three, we both lift up, okay?"

Joey nodded. He bent and took a deep breath.

"One, two, three!"

Joey strained with every muscle. He couldn't raise the crate off the ground. He looked up just in time to see the brawny laborer lift the other end and send it crashing toward his toes. "*Mamma mia!*" Joey jumped back.

"Better go home and practice picking up spaghetti." The laborer grinned, lifted the crate, and tossed it into the freight car.

Joey ran off, his ears burning from the hoots of the freight workers. Dummy, he muttered to himself. Why'd you have to yell out in Italian?

He scuffed along the train tracks saying every swear word he knew in English. He saw a girl pick-

A Place for Joey

ing up coal. Her hair was light, not like the dark hair most kids in the neighborhood had. He bet Luigi would think she was pretty. He had noticed Luigi looking at girls even though he never talked to them. "Hey, leave some coal for somebody else!" he yelled.

The girl turned around quickly, then shook her head and smiled shyly. "*Non ci capisco niente.*"

"Never mind," Joey answered in English, even though she had just said she didn't understand the language. "You should speak English," he said. "You're in America now."

"America," the girl said with a heavy accent.

"The North End. Boston, Massachusetts," Joey said. "If you learn English you can get a good job here. I'm gonna get a job today no matter what."

The girl smiled.

"Not picking up two-hundred-pound crates, though. Bet those guys don't even make twelve bucks a week. I wouldn't work there or at the molasses tank if they begged me."

The girl shrugged and smiled again. Joey strolled back toward the tank. There was just one man outside the pumping station. He was dressed in overalls and a shirt with rolled-up sleeves. Not the guy he and Domenic had seen the other day. He was looking toward the harbor. "Hi, mister," Joey said. "Nice day, huh?"

The guy turned to Joey and grinned. "Forty degrees in January is pretty warm to me." He pointed toward the tanker where men in heavy coats and woolen hats scurried around the deck. "I was just thinking those poor saps out there are freezing to death. They can't wait to get this tank filled and get outta here. Back to Cuba."

Joey pulled off his cap and stuffed it in his pocket. "Yeah, back to Cuba," he said. He had never heard of Cuba, but this guy was friendly. Joey figured maybe he'd know where he could get a job. "How much molasses is in there, anyway?" he asked, stretching his neck to look up at the tank and pretending he really cared.

"Two million gallons when these clowns get done pumping."

"Wow!" Joey stepped forward. "I need a job, mister. Know where I can get one?"

The guy rolled his eyes. "Maybe you ain't heard it, you little Eye-talian, but there's veterans of the Great War looking for jobs. Any jobs there is here go to Americans."

Joey dug his fists into his pockets and backed away. I'm an American, he wanted to say, but the words wouldn't come out. He jumped out of the way of a couple of wagons, then walked slowly across Commercial Street, avoiding the horse manure. He was sure he hadn't slipped and said anything to the man in Italian. Or had he?

"I gotta get a job. I gotta stay in the North End with Domenic," Joey muttered to himself. "I'm gonna show everybody they can't push me around!"

He kicked a tin can savagely with his boot. "I'm not gonna talk Italian ever again," he vowed.

Chapter Four

"HERE'S YOUR BROTHER," Mama said. She was holding Rosa on her lap when Joey came into the house after school the next day. "Now he'll teach us what he learned."

Joey blew out a deep breath. Good thing he didn't skip school today. Mama was in a happy mood, he could tell. Sometimes when Papa and Luigi went away overnight to work for a few days, like they did this morning, she relaxed a bit. Maybe it was because it was January and they were still working. Or maybe it was because she could stay in bed until five o'clock in the morning.

"Domenic's mother said to ask you to come over for a cup of coffee," Joey said.

His mother put Rosa on the floor and stirred the big kettle of clothes on the stove. "I've got too much to do to be gossiping with the neighbors all day," she said.

Joey sighed. She always said the same thing. Mama just wasn't like the other mothers. He knew better than to argue. He sat at the table and opened his writing tablet. "Okay, then I'm gonna give you an English lesson," he said. He rapped his pencil on the table. "Attention!" He tried to sound like his teacher.

Mama gave Rosa a clothespin to play with and sat down across the table. "I'm listening."

"Speak English, please. What is your name?"

Mama tapped her fingers on her head. "My name is Lucia Calabro. I have tree childrens. Names are Luigi, Giuseppe, and Rosa," she said slowly.

Joey shook his head. "Say *three*, Mama. Three, three, three," he repeated. "Their American names are Louie, Joey, and Rosy."

Mama made a face. "That's not what the priest baptized you," she said. "That's not what I said when I went in front of the judge to be an American. He gave me the papers, didn't he?"

Joey waved his hands. He'd heard a million times about how his parents went to classes to become American citizens. "Americans speak English," he said. He rapped on the table again. "Say something else. In English."

"Ooh. You so smart, you boss your mama around now? You so much the boss justa like me when . . ." She reached up to the shelf over the table where a framed picture from Italy stood. She pointed to the girl in the white dress and said in Italian, "I was nine years old when my father had this photograph made. I wanted to wear my new dress and my mother wanted me to wear my communion dress. I stamped my foot and said I was going to wear the new dress or I wouldn't be in the picture." She pushed the wooden frame across the table to Joey and said, "See, I didn't look so happy after my father told me what would happen if I ever bossed my mother around again." She smiled and said in English, "So you teach me but no like boss. Okay?"

"That's very good, Mama," Joey said. "If you speak more in English you'll be almost as good as me."

"That's too much for today. It make my head hurt." Mama got up, moved the big kettle to the back of the stove and reached for a cook pot. "I need to make some gravy for when your father and brother come home."

"Say that in English, Mama," Joey said. "Then when Papa and Luigi come home you can give them lessons. You can be the teacher like me."

"Poor Luigi and your father are too tired from working twelve hours a day on the construction jobs to have English lessons," Mama said.

Joey leaned forward. "Mr. Bonano speaks English. He only works eight hours a day in the restaurant," he said.

"My sons no gonna be waiters!" Mama yelled in English. Then she spoke slowly in Italian. "Mr. Bonano is a good man, Guiseppe, but in our family we don't believe in working for somebody else. Like my father, we're going to own our own farm."

Joey made a face. "I don't wanna own a farm," he said. "I keep telling you I wanna stay here in the North End. I wanna get a good job. I wanna make money."

Mama waggled her finger at him. "Money, money, money! Money no good if you gotta work for some boss alla time. No have nothing for your own." She clasped her hands over her heart and spoke rapidly in Italian. "My father died when I was younger than you, Giuseppe. My poor mother had to sell our farm and go to where my uncle lived." She shook her head. "It was in the south of Italy. It was so poor there that nobody had anything. My two little brothers and my mother died in that place."

"You met Papa there," Joey said trying to get his mother to smile again.

"Yes." Mama's frown disappeared. "That was the one good thing. I met your father, who is the best man in all the world. We had Luigi, you, and Rosa, who are all healthy. I thank God for that every day when I pray. I thank God and St. Francis that pretty soon we'll have our own farm just like in the good times in Italy. We'll have respect. And you and Luigi and Rosa will have babies that are healthy from growing up on a farm."

"I'm healthy and I have good times here in the North End, Mama. I don't wanna move away from here," Joey repeated.

"I no wanna! I no wanna!" Mama yelled and pointed her finger at him. "Until you grow up, you want what your family says! You hear me, Giuseppe? You're too stubborn. Sometimes I think you're too much like me."

"I'm not like anybody," Joey said. He closed the cover of his book. "Can I go over to Domenic's now?"

Mama was still looking at the old picture. "See

the house? See the trees? See all the land behind it? My father owned that land. It was beautiful! It was such a good place."

"Domenic's waiting for me," Joey said.

"You no listen, Giuseppe!" Mama put the picture back on the shelf. "When Luigi was a boy he sat nice and quiet and listened to me." She sighed and waved her hand. "Take your little sister, then, if you have to go out. Put on her coat and button it up good. But first, get me the racks to dry the clothes." She got out the washboard. "In Watertown I'll have a great long clothesline to hang the clothes outside, even in the winter. Imagine, Giuseppe, all the clothes hanging outside in the nice fresh air!"

Joey rolled his eyes. Rosa wiggled and squirmed while he put on her coat. Her sweater hung down below her coat. "You're getting big, Rosy," he said.

His sister looked up at him with wide eyes. "Big," she said.

Mama looked over. "So now Rosa speak English!" She jabbed the wooden spoon in Joey's direction and made a face. "You no teach her to say like you 'I no wanna'!" Mama shoved the spoon in the kettle so hard the water sloshed over and hissed on the top of the stove.

Joey picked up his sister and carried her down

the stairway. When they got to the street, Rosa ran over to the little kids playing in the next doorway. Joey sat on the curbstone.

Domenic came out of the doorway on the other side. When he saw Joey, he grinned and sat beside him. He took a harmonica out of his pocket. "I told you I'd get it. I can play this better than Frankie." He started playing. The little kids came out of the doorway into the street. Two little boys danced to the music. Rosa wedged herself between Joey's legs and jiggled and laughed. A window opened and an old woman looked down at the street and clapped her hands.

"*Grazie!*" she called when Domenic stopped playing.

"*Che bello!* Beautiful!" Mr. Arrico in his white apron came out from the bakery. He held up a large biscotti cookie. "For you, Domenic. Something to make the music sweeter!" Then he looked at Rosa's wide eyes and shrugged his shoulders. He handed her the cookie. "You get one when you play another song," he said to Domenic.

Rosa took a bite of the biscuit and smiled. She held it out to Joey. He took a bite. "Good," he said, inhaling the sweet flavor.

"Good," his little sister repeated.

Joey smiled. He looked up at the old woman in

the window of the tenement building, at the shop-keepers standing in the doorways, and at the kids dancing in the street to Domenic's tarantella. I don't care what Mama says, he thought. This neighborhood, this place right here is *my* good place.

Joey knew the heavy lump in his throat didn't come from Mr. Arrico's biscotti.

Chapter
Five

"THE NEW TEACHER DIDN'T SAY ANYTHING yesterday about my hooking school," Joey said as he and Domenic walked down Salem Street Wednesday morning.

His friend still looked worried. "But what if Miss Peabody is back today? She likes you. She'll probably go to your house to see if you're sick."

Joey pretended he hadn't worried about that. He shrugged his shoulders. "What do I care?"

Domenic put his face up close to Joey's. "What's the matter with you? You're acting crazy in the head."

"No, I'm not," Joey said. "Domenic, I'm gonna tell you a secret. I'm gonna leave school and get a job."

Domenic sat down on the curb and put his head in his hands. Then he looked up and scratched his black curls. "What will I tell your mother? She'll come to my house looking for you." He rolled his eyes. "I'm scared of your mother more than I am my mother." He stood up, put his hand on Joey's shoulder and said, "I know why you're saying that. You don't wanna move to Watertown. I don't want you to move away, either. You're my friend. But don't worry about it so much. My father says your family just has dreams, that's all. My father says it costs too much money to buy land."

Joey couldn't tell Domenic that his family's dreams were about to come true. He couldn't tell about all the money Mama had saved. That was family business. He punched Domenic's arm and tried to smile. "Hey, forget what I say. I just don't want to go to school today. It's a nice day out."

"Yeah," Domenic agreed, still frowning. "I'd hook with you, Joey, only my mother—"

"I know what your mother will say," Joey interrupted. He posed like the prizefighter whose picture was in the window of the saloon down by the waterfront. "I'm gonna kill you, Domenic Bonano!"

He heard his friend laugh. "See you later," Joey yelled as he ran around the corner and up Hull

Street. He paused at the top of the hill. Where will I go first? he asked himself. I gotta think about this. He took a deep breath, turned into the old cemetery and sank down on the ground. He wasn't afraid to go into the graveyard in the bright sunshine. It wasn't like the time he and some of the kids came up here one night last summer. Joey shivered a little thinking about how they all acted so brave until the older kids started telling ghost stories.

"There's underground tunnels in cemeteries so the dead people can wander around at night," one big kid had said. "If you put your ear to the ground, you can hear them walking around."

"Aaah!" Joey remembered how they all screamed, how the goose bumps came out on his arms, and how he and Domenic had covered their ears so they wouldn't hear any footsteps from the dead.

Another kid said that when people died in Sicily, their photographs were put on the graves.

Then Nicky Falco had yelled, "Hey, Domenic, what's your picture doing on that grave over there?"

Joey smiled to himself remembering how fast Domenic had run home, and how later they'd stood laughing together under the safety of the lamppost on Prince Street until their mothers called them inside.

What would summer nights and days be like in Watertown without any friends to pal around with? Joey looked down the hill to North End Park and the barge that he and Domenic swam out to on hot days. He thought about playing stickball and kick-the-can in the street while the grown-ups sat and chatted. He closed his eyes against the sun. I could fall asleep right here, he thought. Then he opened his eyes and blinked. Hey, he said to himself, I gotta get going if I'm gonna get a job. He stood up, then stopped when he heard a voice coming from behind a headstone farther down the hill. That voice doesn't sound like a ghost, he thought. Maybe there's worse things than ghosts. If there's Irish kids hanging out here, I'm in trouble. He ducked behind the nearest headstone and listened. The voice continued. Only one voice. Then he heard the words, spoken haltingly, singsong, sounded out, like when Miss Peabody called on kids to read out loud at school.

"It-was-the-schoon-er-Hes-per-us,
  That-sailed-the-wintry-sea;"

Joey silently crept to the next headstone. That poem was in his school reader. It was about a shipwreck. The voice continued:

"And-the-skip-per-had-taken-his-little-daughter,
  To-keep-him-com-pa-ny."

Joey bent down and quietly slithered down the hill toward the voice.

"Blue-were-her-eyes-as-the-fairy-flax,
Her-cheeks-like-the-dawn-of-day . . ."

The voice droned on. Joey peered over the slab. He clapped his hand over his mouth to keep from laughing. But it was too late. He'd made a noise.

"Get the hell outta here!" It was the red-haired Irish kid who had pushed him against the wall only a few days ago. He dropped a tattered book and jumped up from the grass. There was a half-eaten sandwich still in his big hand. "Whaddaya doing spying on me?"

"I no spy on you," Joey said. "I hear you saying a poem, that's all."

"You didn't hear me saying nothing!" The kid kicked the book behind him. "You just better shut up and scram before I make hamburg outta you!" He moved his foot backward again and tried to cover the book with the brown paper bag on the ground. His face was as red as his hair, which stuck up in unruly cowlicks.

Joey looked at the kid's flushed face and then stared at the book. "We read that book in school," he said, sounding braver than he felt. "The *McGuffey's Reader*. In the front it says Property of the City of Boston."

"So? I found the dumb book. Someone must have swiped it." The redhead took a bite from his thick sandwich. "I was just gonna throw it away," he mumbled.

You're a liar, Joey said to himself. He took a deep breath, pointed to the harbor, and said, "I'm going down there. I'll throw it in the water for you."

The redhead kept his foot on the book. "Just mind your own business and forget you ever saw me, if you know what's good for you." He bent down and put what was left of his sandwich in the bag. Joey saw him slide the *McGuffey's Reader* in the bag as well.

"Whatta I care if you and and your friend Sully like poems?" Joey said. He watched the red fade from the Irish kid's face, replaced by a white pallor that made his freckles stand out in brown patches. He's scared of Sully, Joey thought. He doesn't want him to know. Joey felt a surge of power. Drawing another deep breath, he said, "You know my friend, the one your friend don't like? Well, him and me we can talk about rhymes when we see Sully again. Like 'Blue were her eyes as the fairy flax.' Thattsa pretty poem."

"Geez, you sneaky little wop!" The redhead shook his head. "Sully and me got better things to do than go after weasels like you."

Joey stood up straight. "Don't call me wop."

The redhead sneered. "Okay, weasel," he said. "Get outta my way. I gotta go to work."

"You gotta job? I'm looking for a job," Joey said.

"Yeah, sure. You're hooking school, weasel." The redhead laughed. "Just watch out for that new cop you swore at in Eye-talian. He's tough. He likes to catch kids hooking school. He even went after me once, but Flaherty, the cop whose beat this was before, told him I was fifteen. Good thing I'm big. He believed Flaherty. Geez, that's all my mother needs. Some truant officer making me quit my job and go back to school."

Joey stared. "Your mother wants you to hook school? How old are you anyway?"

"Thirteen. I been working in the stables since I was twelve. Since my pa died. I'm the oldest. I gotta work." He started walking. "Going to school ain't the worst thing in the world, weasel."

Joey hurried along beside him. "Joey. My name's Joey. I'd work in the stables. You think I can get a job there, Buddy?"

"Buddy? My name ain't Buddy. That's what that cop calls everybody. He don't know nobody yet." The redhead looked down at Joey. "Yeah, you can probably get a job shoveling manure. Five cents an hour."

"Where's the stable?" Joey asked.

"Down behind the Public Works Department." The redhead pointed across Commercial Street. "Geez, you're crazy," he said. "I'm telling you, the only job you'll get there is shoveling manure."

"I don't care. I need a job."

The redhead scratched his head. "Hey, you're serious, right? Look, I'll make a deal with you. You can tell Hogan—he's the boss—that you know me. Red O'Neill." He reached out and punched Joey on the shoulder. "But don't talk Eye-talian. Hogan ain't exactly crazy about Eye-talians. And just keep your trap shut about the other stuff if you wanna live. Okay?"

Joey grinned, even though his arm hurt from the punch. "Sure, Red. I keep my trap shut. I won't talk Italian." But I'm never gonna tell you I didn't swear at that cop! he said to himself. Hey! I'm gonna get a job! And no Irish are gonna bother Domenic again!

And he swaggered down the hill.

Chapter Six

J OEY SHADOW-BOXED HIS WAY to Commercial Street. Wait'll I tell Domenic, he thought, grinning to himself and feeling six feet tall. Pow! Bam! No stopping Joey Calabro now! He jabbed a fist in the air.

"Hey! Aren't you the same kid I caught hanging around here before?" Joey felt a hand grab his jacket sleeve. A large hand at the end of a blue cuff! His heart hammered so loud it drowned out the squeal of the overhead elevated train. The policeman's hand tightened as he stared at Joey. "And I keep thinking I've seen you someplace else as well."

"*No ci capisco.*" Joey could barely hear his own

trembling voice. He likes to catch kids hooking school, Red said. And he thinks you swore at him!

The policeman's face got red. "Don't give me that Eye-talian. You spoke English the last time I saw you," he said. "Yer hooking school again, I wager. I let you off then, but this time I'm going to—"

Joey didn't wait to hear what the cop was going to do. He twisted out of his grasp and dashed across Commercial Street, barely escaping being trampled under the hooves of a horse. The wagon driver's curses mingled with the roar of the train, the shouts of the policeman, and the hoots coming from the men sitting in front of the molasses tank. "Run, you little hooligan!" Joey heard through his pounding ears. He raced into the freight yard, leap-frogged over a bale of leather and two beer barrels and landed on his knees. He looked down at his ripped pants. "*Mamma mia!*" he moaned.

"Relax, kid," a voice said. "That cop gave up once he saw how fast you could run. You practicing for the marathon?"

Joey stood up slowly, brushing gravel from his bare scraped knees. Two freight workers sitting outside were grinning at him.

"I never seen anyone run so fast. You're speedier than Clarence DeMar," the heavy guy said. "What'd you steal to make that cop chase you?"

Joey straightened up. His knees hurt. "I no steal nothing. I was justa . . . " He looked down at his torn pants. "I was just . . . " He shrugged his thin shoulders and sighed.

"Well, stay out of trouble, speedy," the smaller workman said. "We'll be looking for you at the marathon right behind DeMar." He unwrapped his sandwich, turned to his coworker and said, "So, whacha think, Bill? The Red Sox gonna win the World Series again?"

Joey studied his ripped pants. Looking at them made his knees hurt even more. He leaned over, picked up a long piece of wood, and leaned on it. Even hearing that the men thought he ran almost as fast as the great Boston Marathon runner wasn't enough to dispel his fear at what Mama would say when she saw his torn trousers. And that cop was still in the neighborhood. What if he found out where he lived? Came to the house? Joey could see him across the street talking with a woman leaning out of her second-story window. He watched him wave at her and then stroll toward Hanover Street. I'll wait until just before he turns to come back, Joey thought. Then I'll find the stable. His knees still hurt, but he decided he could still run. He ducked behind a freight car and kept his eyes on the policeman.

"*Boungiorno.* Hello," a soft voice said. "*Non fa freddo oggi.* Good day, no?"

Joey turned. The light-haired girl he'd seen before smiled at him. She had a basket half-filled with sticks.

"That's right. It's not cold today. It's nice." Joey forgot his torn pants and smiled. "You listened to me. You're learning English, right?"

The girl shrugged her shoulders, smiled at him again, and said, "Okay."

Joey held out his piece of wood. "You can have this," he said.

The girl shook her head. "*Ma ä troppo grande.*" She held her hands wide apart.

"Too big." Joey said. He wanted to keep talking to her, to tell her about the job he was going to get, but he spotted the policeman almost at the corner. He looked like he was going to cross the street. Aah! If I go to the stable, he'll see me! I better get back up the hill! Joey wished he *had* sworn at the cop!

"I gotta go. Good-bye!" Joey shouted at the girl and dashed across Commercial Street carrying the piece of wood like a balancing pole. The woman in the window of the corner house on Copp's Hill shook her finger at him, but she was smiling. "You better not be hooking school no more," she called down in an Irish accent. "Next time you'll be caught. 'Twas the lucky one you are today, boyo!"

Joey didn't stop running until he reached the top of the hill. Lucky? He didn't think he was lucky. The cop was after him, he ripped his pants, and his mother would be furious. And he'd have to wait for another time to go to the stables. He'd have to check when that cop wasn't around. "I'm lucky like a cockroach is lucky," Joey said aloud. "Only good thing today was meeting Red O'Neill." He stared down at the waterfront. The air was so clear he could pick out the light-haired girl with her basket of kindling. He couldn't see the cop, but he could see beyond the freight buildings. He could see the sailors on a navy ship behind the fireboat at Engine 31. He glanced to the left. Even with the sun reflecting off the molasses tank, he could see the guys out front eating their lunch. Joey's stomach rumbled. He was hungry and too scared to go home with his torn pants. And he had to tell Mama about the job he was going to get. About how he wasn't going to go to Watertown. How he was going to—

Suddenly Joey felt the sidewalk move under his feet like a giant wave. For just a second he had a thought about dead bodies walking under the ground. But then—

RAT-A-TAT! A blast like a machine gun knocked him to the sidewalk. Joey curled into a ball, closed his eyes, and shielded his ears against the horrendous sound. BLAST-BLAST-BLAST! It sounded like the whole world was crashing around him.

"*Aiutami, San Francesco, ti prego!*" Joey prayed.

Just as quickly as they started, the booming noises stopped, replaced by a low roar like the ocean in a northeast storm.

Joey opened one eye. The sun was still shining. He stumbled to his feet. The roaring sound was muffled now, as if the ocean storm was over. He looked down to the waterfront.

"*Mamma mia!*" Joey screamed out in Italian and crossed himself. "It's the end of the world!"

All he could see was twisted, tangled steel, wire, and wooden buildings flattened to the ground. The elevated track hung crazily over the street like a giant pretzel, a train at the very edge of the broken rails. Where the huge molasses tank stood moments before, Joey saw only a wall of thick brown liquid gushing across Commercial Street like a giant wave. He heard the distant wail of sirens. "Oh, my God," he murmured in Italian. "Where are all the people?" Joey made the sign of the cross again, grabbed his stick in his trembling hands and started running down the hill, thinking of the light-haired girl.

Footsteps echoed behind him. He heard voices yelling in Italian and English. "It's the molasses tank! The molasses tank exploded!"

Joey kept running down the hill.

Chapter Seven

WHEN JOEY REACHED THE BOTTOM of the hill he couldn't run anymore. His shoes were mired in gloppy goo. It reached his ankles. He looked frantically around. Where was the house on the corner where the Irish lady just called out to him? It had disappeared like he had only dreamed it, a heap of rubble in its place. Joey stood like a statue, molasses sucking at his shoes. He stared across the street and saw only piles of wood; huge, jagged pieces of metal; and a foaming, churning lake of molasses. The tank, the city yards, and freight sheds were gone. *Where was the light-haired girl?* He had seen her just a few minutes ago behind the sheds. But all he could see there now were scraps of boards leaning crazily against each other, like matchsticks tossed out of the box. Covered with something that looked like brown, sticky mud. *But it's not mud.* Joey looked down at his feet. *It's molasses!*

The stinking stuff hadn't crept any higher than his ankles. But just in front of him, in the street, the molasses was a foot high. Even more in the middle of the street. Joey felt a rush of helplessness. I can't get across. I can't get to the freight yard. I can't do anything to help that girl. "St. Francis, what can I do?" he cried out in Italian.

Then, amid the sound of sirens wailing in the distance, Joey heard a faint whistle, then a low voice. "Is somebody there, for God's sake?"

Joey spun around at the sound. About two feet in front of him, he spotted a blue-coated arm moving beneath one of the piles of shattered wood and scraps of steel. Molasses lapped around the heap of wreckage. "*Mamma mia!*" Joey shouted.

He heard a low groan. "I ask for help and I get someone who can't understand English! I tink my arm's broken, the molasses is up to me neck like glue, and the smell is making me sick. I tink I'm going to pass out."

Joey tried to stop shaking. He'd last heard that voice threatening him. That blue-coated arm had

grabbed him. What was it he'd said? "*'This time
I'm going to—'*" Thoughts swirled around in Joey's
head. *I know what he was going to do! He was
going to arrest me!*

"For Jaysus' sake, if anybody's there, help me!"
The voice was growing fainter.

Joey wanted to run away. He looked frantically
around. *There must be someone else here but me.
There must be someone!*

There was no one. And the voice in Joey's head
kept telling him in Italian: You have to help.

He tried to yell out, to tell the policeman that he
understood. He'd help. He had to help. But the
English words wouldn't come out. He couldn't
think in English. He could only think in Italian!

"Please don't get sick. Please don't faint. I'm
going to help you." Joey leaned on his stick, lifting
one foot, then the other. He inched forward, keeping
up a steady chatter in Italian as he struggled to move
through the sticky glop. "Don't worry. I'm going to
help you." Joey inched closer and closer, leaning
on his stick, terrified that he'd fall and never be
able to get up. "St. Francis, help me. Help the
policeman!"

He heard the faint voice of the policeman mum-
bling something he couldn't understand. Then he
heard him say, "For God's sake, buddy boy, watch

yerself. If you come any closer, you'll fall in and we'll both drown."

Joey fought to stay on his feet as he pushed his legs against the thick molasses. "I can hear people across the street. I have to get where they can see me. They'll help you!"

Joey heard some more muttering, then a low moan and then silence. "St. Francis, Mary, and Joseph, make him be okay." He labored to reach a spot where he could see beyond the piles of rubble. He could see men jumping out of fire engines, and trucks with red crosses. He heard yelling and saw them start to dig frantically in the wreckage of the firehouse across the street.

He waved his arms and screamed. "*Aiuto, aiuto! Il poliziotto ci sta qua!*"

Joey saw two men look his way. Then they turned away.

They can't understand me! Joey prayed like he'd never prayed before. "St. Francis, give me the words!" He yelled again. "Help! Help! Over here! Mr. Policeman! He's under here!" He pointed toward the pile of rubble.

"We see you! We're coming!"

"They're coming, Mr. Policeman. Please don't die," Joey pleaded as a dozen men carrying long poles slogged and slipped their way through the river of molasses covering Commercial Street. "St. Francis, please, please, let them save the policeman and I'll never ask for anything, ever again! I'll be a good boy. I'll go to Watertown. I'll mind Mama."

"Under there," he pointed as the men came closer. "Mr. Policeman!" With the aid of his stick Joey moved slowly backward in the muck until only his shoes were covered with molasses. He stood by, watching, until he saw the long, still form of the policeman pulled out and put on a stretcher. He looked like a ghost—a ghost covered with slimy, sickening gore. Joey turned and struggled up the hill, blinded by tears that wouldn't stop.

Chapter Eight

At the top of the hill the world was normal, except for the crowd of kids, mothers, and storekeepers gathered on Sheafe and Hull Streets. Voices raised, they chattered, pointing, and peering at the wreckage below.

All Joey heard were a few words in the babble.

"Ooh, it's Joey Calabro! Look at him!"

"Joey, you all right? What were you doing down there? Your mama's looking for you!"

Joey ignored the shouts and brushed off attempts to wipe off his clothes. He took off his shoes and socks, ran down Prince Street, and stumbled up the stairs to his house.

He sat at the kitchen table dressed only in his long underwear. He wrapped the gray blanket closer around him as he watched Mama slosh his trousers, shirt, and socks in the big kettle.

"Phew! Such a stink!" Mama held her nose and smiled at him.

Joey didn't smile back. He couldn't. But he couldn't tell Mama about why he kept crying, either.

She came over and wrapped him in her arms.

"Guisppe, you think only little boys get scared when they hear such a big bang? I thought it was the Germans bombing us." She shivered. "Such a loud noise! BOOM!"

Mama kept telling him how frightened everyone in the neighborhood had been, how they all ran outside, and how finally Domenic's big brother had come and told them that the tank had exploded. "Frankie says Commercial Street is covered five feet deep in molasses. And my Giuseppe's not home. My God! If you knew how scared you make me!" Mama hugged him again. "The neighbors say people were swallowed up and drowned by the molasses before they even knew what happened."

Joey wanted Mama to keep hugging him but to stop talking about people getting killed. He didn't want to think about that. When he closed his eyes, he kept seeing the light-haired girl, the Irish lady, and the policeman. He kept hearing himself unable to remember any English, babbling away to the policeman in Italian like Mama was babbling to him now.

"You shouldn't have gone down there to see what happened," Mama continued. "You should have come right home after school." She scraped his shoes with a brush.

Joey jumped when he heard a *rap, rap* on the door. Domenic burst in.

"Joey! I've been looking for you all over! Somebody told me—" He stopped, took off his cap, and looked at Joey's mother. "Hello, Mrs. Calabro."

Mama waved her hand. "Hallo." She turned to Joey. "See, Domenic came home after school like a good boy. He doesn't make his mother's hair turn white with worry. You hear me, Guisseppe?"

"I hear you, Mama." Finally the English words came out—when it was too late, when he couldn't comfort the policeman who was dying. Joey wiped his nose with the blanket.

"Domenic, you stay here with Giuseppe while I go across to the grocer's, all right? Rosa is sleeping."

Domenic sat down at the table. "Sure, Mrs. Calabro." As soon as she left, he leaned across the table. "Where were you when the explosion came, Joey? I was so scared. I thought you were . . . "

Joey shook his head. He sniffed. "I was up on the hill."

"But everybody said you were all covered with molasses," Domenic said. "Did you go down there? People got killed, they said. Did you see ?"

Joey picked at the lint on the blanket. "I don't want to talk now."

His friend frowned, scratched his head, then nodded. "Sure, Joey. That's all right by me." He looked at Joey's ruined shoes. "Uh, oh, I bet your mother killed you for ruining your clothes, right?"

Joey hunched his shoulders. "She didn't say anything."

Domenic scratched his head again.

◆ ◆ ◆

Joey lay on his cot, trying to sleep. Trying to erase the images that wouldn't go away. The light from the kerosene lamp shone on a dark, cracked patch of plaster on the ceiling. Before his eyes it turned into molasses surging across Commercial Street, swallowing everything in its evil path. But if he closed his eyes, it was worse. He could see the light-haired girl stooping over to pick up some kindling. Did she even have a chance to look up when she heard the terrible explosion, or did the angry wave cover her before she could . . . ? Joey pulled the gray blanket over his head. But the horrible images crept under the blanket with him. Ghosts, covered with brown slime. "Aaah!" Joey let out a cry.

He heard footsteps. "Giuseppe? Are you all right?"

"Yes, Mama," Joey lied. "I had a bad dream."

"A dream you want to tell me?"

"No, Mama," Joey lied again. How could he talk to Mama about what he didn't even want to think about?

"Go to sleep then, Giuseppe."

"Yes, Mama."

He closed his eyes tight. He'd do what Mama said.

The next morning Mama brought out his church clothes.

"You'll have to wear these to school. I still have to scrub some more and sew your pants from yesterday." She smoothed his black church pants. "Don't get these dirty, you hear me, Giuseppe?"

"Yes, Mama," Joey answered. He numbly pulled his clothes on, then drank the coffee and ate the bread Mama put before him. He walked slowly down the stairs. Even his good shoes felt heavy, as if he were still struggling in the molasses. His stomach churned when he smelled the sickly sweet aroma still in the air.

A Place for Joey

Domenic came out of his doorway. He crinkled his nose, then looked over at Joey and whistled. "Hey, you look pretty swell." His eyes lit up. "So, what was it like down there, Joey? Frankie said the whole tank exploded and people were drowned in the molasses. He said horses were like statues covered in molasses. He said—"

"Stop!" Joey shook his head. He wanted to tell Domenic what happened—every horrible nightmarish minute of the hell on Commercial Street. But like yesterday, when the English words wouldn't come out to comfort the policeman as he lay dying, today no words at all would come out except, "I don't wanna talk about it."

Domenic frowned and tugged his hair. After a few minutes he poked Joey and said, "Guess what? I beat Frankie playing checkers last night. Whattya think of that?"

"Good," Joey said.

Domenic kept looking at Joey as they walked in silence down the street. Finally he snapped his fingers. "Hey, you wanna hear a funny story about this fancy-dressed lady who came into my father's restaurant the other day?"

Joey shrugged. "I don't care."

Domenic stopped. "You're gonna like this one, Joey. Honest. See, this lady, she acts like she's somebody, you know, and this is what she says to my father." Domenic twirled his finger and mimicked in a high-pitched voice. " 'Ooh, I'm soooo weary from shopping all day! I'd like some tea and something sweet.' She looks at the menu and says. 'I think I'll have the sweetbreads.' My father, he can tell she doesn't know what sweetbreads are, so he says, real nice, 'We have some delicious cream pie today, Miss. Maybe you'd like to have that instead.' But this lady, she says in a snooty voice, 'I said I want sweetbreads.' My father says 'Okay, Miss, whatever you want,' and when he brings the plate," Domenic bent over and laughed so hard he couldn't talk. "I think I'm gonna pee my pants!"

Joey grinned. "What did she do?"

Domenic straightened up and grinned back. "She says, 'Waiter, this isn't what I ordered.' My father says real polite again, 'It's what you ordered, Miss. Sweetbreads.' The lady picks up her fork and takes a bite. 'Well, it's good, but it certainly doesn't look or taste like any sweet bread I've ever had,' she says. My father says to her, 'Well, you see, Miss, sweetbreads aren't bread.' The lady kind of waves him off, looks at him like he's dumb or something, and says, 'It's all right, waiter. It tastes very good.' So my father just smiles back and walks away. He comes back over to the table when the lady's almost finished and says, 'I'm glad you're enjoying the *mogliadelli.*' The lady says, 'Oh, is that what Italians call sweet pastry?' My father just smiles and says, 'No, Miss, it's what we call sweet-breads—what you're eating. It's the inside of a cow.' The lady drops her fork, screams, and throws up!"

Joey couldn't help it. He burst out laughing.

Domenic grinned and punched him on the shoulder.

Domenic talked all the way home from school as well. He talked about everything except the molasses tank explosion. "I'll bring my checker-board over and teach you how I beat Frankie," he said when they got to his tenement.

Joey bent over to tie his shoelace. "Maybe I'll beat you," he said. In spite of being so tired, he'd paid attention to Miss Peabody this morning. "I did good in arithmetic today." It was easy not to think of anything else if he concentrated on the lesson.

Domenic grinned. "You don't have to be good in arithmetic to play checkers. You just gotta be a genius like me. I, uh, oh . . . "

"Whattsa matter?" Joey looked up. He saw a crowd on the sidewalk in front of his house. Mama was standing there with Rosa by her side. Joey felt his legs sway, and put out his hand and pressed it against the side of Domenic's tenement.

Chapter Nine

MAMA LOOKED OVER AND SAW HIM. "Giuseppe! Come here! What did you do? The policeman is looking for you!"

Joey stared beyond Mama at one of the ghosts he'd seen all night. But this ghost was alive. His left arm was bandaged. His mustache was shaved off. But he was alive and he was talking. To him.

"I've been walking around here all morning looking for someone." Joey heard the policeman's deep voice. "People tell me a kid named Joey Calabro came home covered in molasses yesterday. Is yer name Joey Calabro?"

Joey nodded.

"Do you speak English?"

Joey nodded again.

"I'd like to hear you say something."

Joey looked around. Mama had her dark eyes fixed on him. Domenic was staring. Mr. Venezia and Mr. Russo were outside their markets peering across the street. Women were standing on the sidewalk with their black net grocery bags over their arms. It seemed to Joey that the whole neighborhood was there on Prince Street watching him. He said a silent prayer of thanks to St. Francis that the policeman wasn't dead. Then he looked at him and said, "I'm sorry I hooked school, Mr. Policeman. I no do it no more."

The policeman laughed. "Yer the one I was looking for, Joey Calabro." He put his good arm around Joey's shoulder and said in a loud voice, "This boyo saved my life yesterday."

Joey heard the swell of voices in English and Italian. "Joey saved the policeman's life! Giuseppe saved the policeman's life!"

Neighbors crowded around, asking what Joey Calabro did.

Joey stared at the policeman. He's alive, he kept saying to himself. He's alive!

"I was a goner for sure," he heard the deep voice say. "Knocked off me feet and buried alive in the stinking molasses. There I was, saying me Act of Contrition, praying to God to forgive me my sins, and along comes a boy, talking to me in words I don't understand. First, I'm in despair of me life, but then it comes to me he's saying prayers and helping me and the words I don't understand sound like the voice of an angel. I niver heard anything so beautiful in my life, and I'm dying peaceful and content."

The policeman smiled. "But I didn't die at all, did I? The next thing I know, I wake up in the Red Cross tent. They're telling me that if it wasn't for this Italian kid yelling something about 'Mr. Policeman,' I'd be facing me Maker, leaving a widow and five kids to struggle on their own." The policeman dabbed at his eyes.

"How many die?" Mr. Russo from the meat market asked, after the murmurs of voices had finished translating the story.

The policeman shook his head sadly. "Last I heard it was a dozen or so dead. There'll be more when they get the mess all cleaned out." He tightened his hand on Joey's shoulder. "Then there's hundreds injured, some a lot worse than me. I just got this broken left arm." He sighed. "Terrible enough about the poor workmen that got killed, but a place in me heart aches for Mrs. Clougherty, whose house blew to kingdom come, and that pretty little Italian girl with the light hair who used to come every day to get coal and wood. They niver knew what happened to them, God rest their souls." He took off his cap and bowed his head.

"God rest their souls," Joey joined the neighbors murmuring in Italian.

The tall man in blue held out his hand. "I want to thank you again, Joey Calabro. You're one of the bravest lads I ever knew, bar none at all. You're a hero and a credit to the Eye-talians in the North End of Boston, you are. You have my eternal respect. The wife and the kiddos say thank you as well."

Joey took the big hand that shook his.

The policeman looked at Mama. "Does your mother know what I'm saying? Does she understand English?"

Joey looked at Mama. He saw the proud smile in her eyes. He nodded. "Sometimes."

Chapter Ten

MAMA DIDN'T SAY ANYTHING when the policeman left except to ask Joey if he wanted to invite Domenic for supper.

"I've got the gravy you like. Maybe Domenic likes it, too," Mama said. She called Rosa over from the bakery where Mr. Arrico was giving out cookies to all the neighbors. "In honor of Joey Calabro," he told everyone.

"Such a fuss today. Rosa will have a stomachache," Mama said, but Joey knew, even without the smile in her eyes, that she understood what Mr. Arrico had said.

"Come, little one. Enough cookies for you."

Mama pointed to the two cookies in Rosa's hand. "Give one to your big brother." She turned to Joey. "You come home and change your clothes after you see Domenic. Do you hear me, Giuseppe?"

"Yes, Mama," Joey said. He took the cookie Rosa gave him and waved back as she kept turning around while Mama led her home.

Suddenly, he felt a tug on his sleeve. "Joey! Get in here!" Domenic pushed him into the narrow doorway of the nearest tenement and squeezed in beside him. "That Irish kid! He's across the street! He's looking for you!"

Joey saw a tall red-haired kid walking toward him. He stepped out onto the sidewalk. "Hi, Red," he said.

"Geez!" Joey heard Domenic whisper from the doorway. "Whaddya doing?"

"Hi ya, weasel," Red O'Neill said with a grin. He gestured toward the waterfront. "Heard you saved that new cop's life yesterday. Sure glad I wasn't around there. I seen what it looked like on Commercial Street today. Cripes, it's like there was a war down there!" Red shook his red head. "Kinda scary, right?"

Joey nodded.

Red pointed at Domenic in the doorway.

"Whattsa matter with him? Looks scared of his own shadow. Bet he'd be too scared to do what you did."

"No, he wouldn't, Red," Joey said. "That's my friend, Domenic. He's not scared of anything."

"Yeah, well, if you say so, that's okay by me," Red said. "Okay by my friends, too." He gave Joey a punch on the shoulder. "Hey, I gotta get moving. Just wanted to say hi to ya, Joey. So long, Domenic." He swaggered off.

"Geez! I don't believe this!" Domenic said, staring. "Geez, Joey!" He banged his fist against his head.

Joey grinned.

◆ ◆ ◆

Joey and Domenic leaned over the checkerboard at the kitchen table after the dishes had been washed and put away. Mama sat sewing, watching them.

"When Papa and Luigi come home tomorrow you can't stay up so late," she said.

"It's only eight o'clock, Mama." Joey yawned as he glanced at the big clock over the stove and moved his black checker.

Domenic clapped his hands and jumped his red checker over Joey's. "King me!" he yelled, jumping up from the chair.

"No fair," Joey said. "Mama was talking to me and—"

"You have to pay attention, Giuseppe, like you tell me," Mama said. "Time for you to go home, Domenic. You won the game."

"But the game's not over, Mrs. Calabro," Domenic said. "You see, when you king somebody, then—"

Mama stood up. "Good night to you, Domenic."

"Oh, okay." Domenic packed up the board and the checkers. "We gotta continue this tomorrow, Joey. You did pretty good for the first time," he said.

"Yeah, I did." Joey yawned again.

Domenic stood on one foot with his checker-board under his arm. "The policeman said Joey's a hero, Mrs. Calabro. The policeman said—"

"I hear what the policeman say." Mama put her arm around Joey's shoulder and squeezed him tight. "Good night, Domenic. My Giuseppe is tired."

◆ ◆ ◆

Joey listened to the sounds of Mama bustling around the kitchen. Then he heard a chair creak, a sigh, and the scratchy sound of her sewing box being opened.

"Mama?"

"Go to sleep, Giuseppe. It's nine o'clock already."

"Mama, can Domenic come visit when we move to Watertown?"

Joey heard nothing but the creaking chair for a few minutes. Then Mama spoke in a soft voice, "I thought you didn't want to go to Watertown?"

"That was before. Things are different now." I made a promise to St. Francis, Joey said to himself. He couldn't go back on that now.

"So? Things change when you grow up. Nothing stays the same except what you see and hear in your heart."

Joey listened to the clock ticking and the chair creaking and then to his thoughts. It was hard to find what was in his heart when the feelings there were all mixed up. Things had changed, as Mama said. Did that mean he was grown up?

Joey pictured his good place—his North End neighborhood. He saw the narrow streets filled with wagons and pushcarts. He heard people talking and laughing. He saw himself, laughing, chasing Domenic through the streets. He smelled the aromas from the bakery, the grocery, and the meat market. All those things were in his head and in his heart. Then he saw the place beyond his neighborhood, where people didn't listen to other people. Where he got called names.

But I did okay in that other place, Joey thought.

I got Red O'Neill to listen to me. He's not gonna call me wop anymore. And he didn't have to, but he was gonna help me get a job. And the policeman, he said I was a credit to the North End. Joey listened to the voices in his heart. He heard voices in Italian, and he heard voices in English. And he understood them both.

He guessed the policeman understood them both, too. Now. He said that this afternoon. At first he didn't hear anything but some words he didn't know. He was as scared as me, Joey thought. But then he listened. He knew I was trying to help him.

I did help him, Joey told himself. I'm not a hero, but I did a good thing. Suddenly, Joey recognized all the places in his head and in his heart.

He got up from the cot and stood at the kitchen table. "Mama, I got something I wanna say."

"You don't have to say anything," Mama said.

"Yes, I do, Mama," Joey said. "I wanna tell you what happened yesterday, how come I was down on Commercial Street when the flood came. How come I hooked school and—"

"Ssh! You wait and tell Papa and Luigi when they come home tomorrow, Guiseppe. Sometimes I don't always understand what a boy does."

Joey looked at Mama in surprise. She wasn't mad at him. He knew that. Sometimes I don't understand you either, Mama, he thought. Even when we speak the same language.

"But I wanna tell you. I'm gonna go with you and Papa and Luigi to Watertown. I'll work hard on the farm." Joey took a deep breath. "But I got something else I want to tell you, too. Someday, I'm gonna come back here. To the North End."

He watched Mama slowly draw the needle through her mending. "I'm listening to you, Guiseppe," she said.

"I don't wanna work in a restaurant, Mama," Joey said quickly. "And I don't want to shovel manure. I don't wanna work on construction, either. I wanna help people." He took a deep breath. "I wanna be a policeman. It'd be good to have a policeman who speaks Italian and English, don't you think? I could help people who don't speak English. I could help people to understand what people say in Italian. Some things mostly mean the same in English and Italian, you know, if you listen. I'd listen." Joey took a deep breath. "Whaddya think, Mama? Being a policeman is a respectable job, isn't it?"

Mama wrinkled her forehead. "An Italian policeman? I never heard of an Italian policeman in America." She raised her hands. "Ooh, Guiseppe, you have a big, big dream!"

"Can I do it, Mama?"

Mama shrugged her shoulders. "How can I tell you what you can do in your dream, Guiseppe?"

Joey smiled. "Then I *can* come back here? I won't have to stay on the farm forever and raise vegetables like Papa and Luigi?"

Mama folded her arms. "When you get as old as your brother you ask me again."

"But Luigi's twenty." Joey counted on his fingers. "It'll be eight years till I'm twenty!"

Mama unwrapped her arms and looked at him. "Eight years is not forever, Guiseppe. A big dream is worth waiting for." She smiled. "How do you say that in English, anyway?"

Joey climbed back on his cot. "It's the same," he said. "You waited a long time for your dream to come true, didn't you, Mama?"

Mama nodded. "I had to wait until I was an old lady." She tucked the gray blanket over Joey's legs and smiled. "But not you. People will see my son when he's twenty and say, 'Ooh, look at that good, smart young policeman who helps everybody in the city!'" She brushed the dark hair from Joey's forehead. "Good night, Guiseppe. Sweet dreams to you."

"Good night, Mama."

Seven years since he'd come here to the North

End, Joey thought. Eight years and he'd be back here again. For good. It was a long, long time. But he'd be a policeman someday, he knew he would. He'd help make his good place even better. He'd help make America better.

Joey turned over on his narrow cot. He had a lot to do before then. He had to finish school. And there was the Calabro Farm—Mama's dream. And Papa's and Luigi's, too. That would take a lot of work. But he could still come back and visit Domenic. And, in the summers, Domenic could come and visit. He could help Joey pick the beets, beans, broccoli, and Papa's swiss chard. Then they could go down to that river in Watertown and swim. Maybe they could build a boat.

He had lots of things to tell Domenic tomorrow. And lots of questions to ask the policeman. How old did you have to be to join the police? Maybe Mama would let him come back in four years, when he was sixteen. Would he be the first Italian-American policeman in Boston?

Joey heard the rocking chair creak. He heard coins clinking. He got up and peeked around the curtain.

Mama was counting the money in the jar. She had a smile on her face. He watched while she put the jar back on the shelf, then reached over and touched the picture from Italy. She smiled, shook her head, and murmured, "Imagine! My son a policeman in America!" Then she turned down the kerosene lamp.

Joey climbed back on the cot and closed his eyes. All these plans were making him sleepy. He turned over and pulled the gray blanket up to his neck.

"Sweet dreams to you, too, Mama," Joey called out softly in Italian.

Author's Note

A *Place for Joey* is a work of fiction inspired by true stories of Italian immigrants who fled the poverty of southern Italy in the early 1900s. Many of these newcomers settled in the North End of Boston, which had already seen an influx of immigrants from Eastern Europe and Ireland. Language and customs sometimes created tension among ethnic groups as they all sought freedom from the oppression and poverty of their homelands. Dreams of freedom came in differing languages, but, as Joey Calabro discovered, they all were about the same thing—the pursuit of the American dream.

There actually was a molasses "flood" in Boston in 1919. Twenty-one people lost their lives, and hundreds more were injured. But in Boston today many people have never heard of the bizarre North End disaster. Headlines of the day in local papers told of "panic among the foreign populations of the North End," but later stories told of heroism from all ethnic groups.

There was no Joey Calabro who saved an Irish policeman's life, but there were at least two immigrant children who perished, including a young "fair-haired Italian girl," who was gathering wood in the freight yard when the tank exploded. Many more survived due to the heroic work of policemen, firemen, and rescue crews, who saw not nationalities but people in distress.

The North End today is still primarily an Italian-American neighborhood. Tourists and Bostonians of all backgrounds enjoy wandering the narrow streets and savoring the aromas and delicacies from many small restaurants.

This story is for all immigrants who found their dream and for those who are still seeking.